Copyright © 2018 Scott Books 34

All rights reserved. No part of this publication may be reproduced, distributed, or transmitted in any form or by any means, including photocopying, recording, or other electronic or mechanical methods, without the prior written permission of the publisher, except in the case of brief quotations embodied in critical reviews and certain other noncommercial uses permitted by copyright law. For permission requests, write to the publisher, addressed "Attention: Permissions Coordinator," at the address below.

ISBN: 978-0-692-19289-4 (Paperback)

ISBN: 978-1-7923-0166-7 (Electronic Book)

Any references to historical events, real people, or real places are used fictitiously. Names, characters, and places are products of the author's imagination.

Front cover image by Sara Luckhardt.

Book design by Eric Scott.

First printing edition 2018.

P.O. Box 167272
Oregon, OH 43616

https://scottbooks34.wixsite.com/mysite

www.scottbooks34.@gmail.com

About Dr. Shurney

Dr. Wanda Whitten-Shurney serves as the CEO and Medical Director of the Sickle Cell Disease Association of America, Michigan Chapter. She has spent 28 years providing compassionate care for children living with sickle cell disease in the Comprehensive Sickle Cell Clinic at Children's Hospital of Michigan. She serves on the Legislative Committee for the reauthorization of the Sickle Cell Disease and Other Heritable Blood Disorders Treatment Act 2018 and the Medical and Research Advisory Committee for the National SCDAA which was co-founded by her late father, Dr. Charles Whitten, a leader in sickle cell research and medical practitioner. Dr. Shurney was the driving force in establishing the Sickle Cell Donor Program for the American Red Cross of Southeastern Michigan and was recently appointed to the National Heart Lung and Blood Institute's Advisory Committee for sickle cell disease.

Introduction

Kids and adults have many questions about sickle cell disease. Many people may not understand what their family members or friends are experiencing, and the complications related to the disease. "What Dr. Shurney Taught Me," is an introductory book about what you or your loved ones might experience when dealing with sickle cell disease. The goal is to reach all audiences with real experiences and educational information about the disease. Each case varies from patient to patient and this book is not intended to replace the expertise of the healthcare providers who specialize in sickle cell disease. However, this book will help you better understand sickle cell disease. If you have any specific questions, please consult with your nearest healthcare provider.

Dedication

*This Book is dedicated to
Dr. Wanda Whitten-Shurney and her late father
Dr. Charles Whitten for all their hard work dealing
with sickle cell disease.*

*This book is also dedicated to all the sickle cell warriors who
continue to show strength, passion, dedication, and
determination to fight a constant battle of pain and fatigue.*

Mommy and Daddy both gave off a sickle gene when they made me, and whenever my fever goes over 101 degrees, we must go get a room at the emergency.

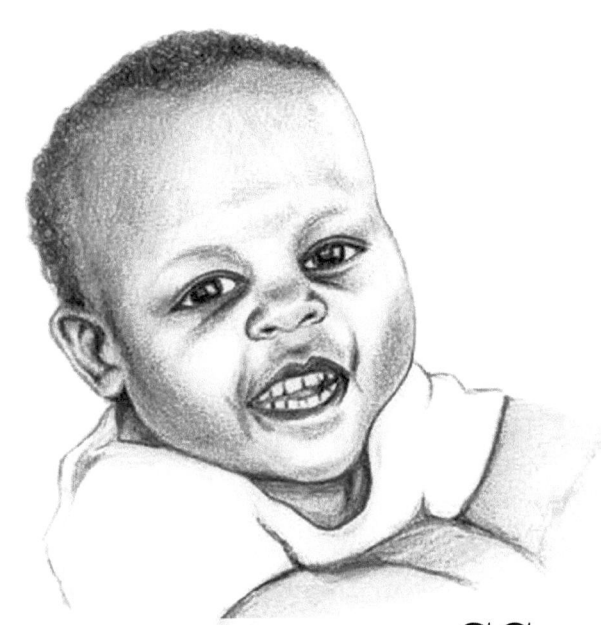

Doctors take pictures of my chest and look up at my nose. They listen to my back and put a beeping thing on my toes.

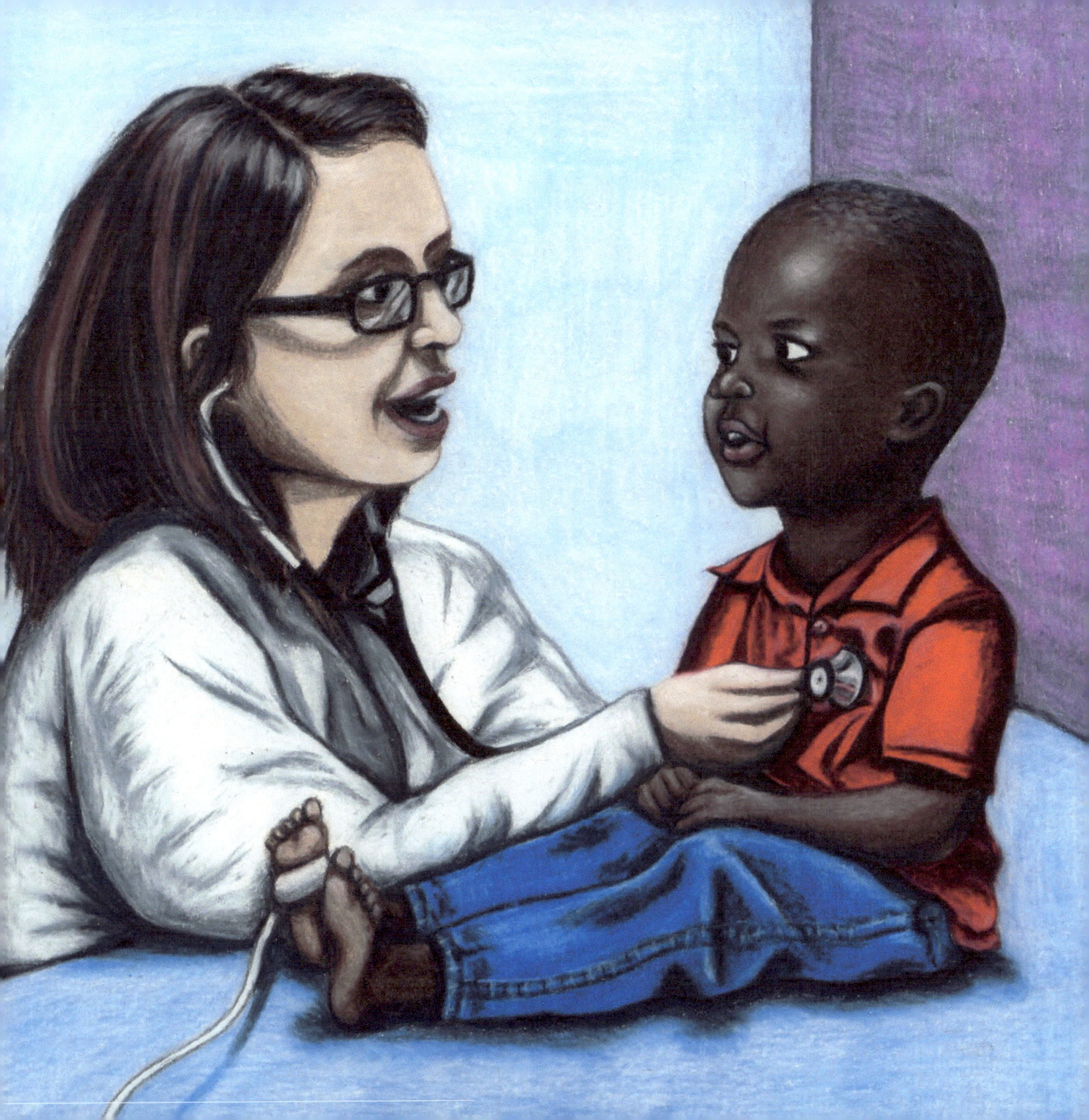

I can go home if after 48 hours I'm ok. But if I still have a fever or am sick, I must stay. This is to help keep me safe.

I get 2.5ml of pink medicine twice a day and I drink it right up, daddy says it will help fight off bacteria. So, bacteria you better leave or be out of luck.

Sickle cell is a disease that turned my normal round blood cells into shapes like the crescent moon. All types of people get the disease, so I have faith a cure will be found soon.

Normal Red Blood Cells

Sickled Red Blood Cells

When it's too hot, I must stay cool. So, in the summertime, I spend many days in the pool.

Also, in the summertime, it's easy for me to get dehydrated and very thirsty, but mommy and daddy give me plenty of fluids and that's fine with me.

My joints hurt sometimes. My mommy rubs me down and tells me everything will be fine. Warm baths and medicine will help, but they may take some time.

If it gets too cold, I stay indoors to keep warm. I don't mind because we get to watch movies and eat popcorn.

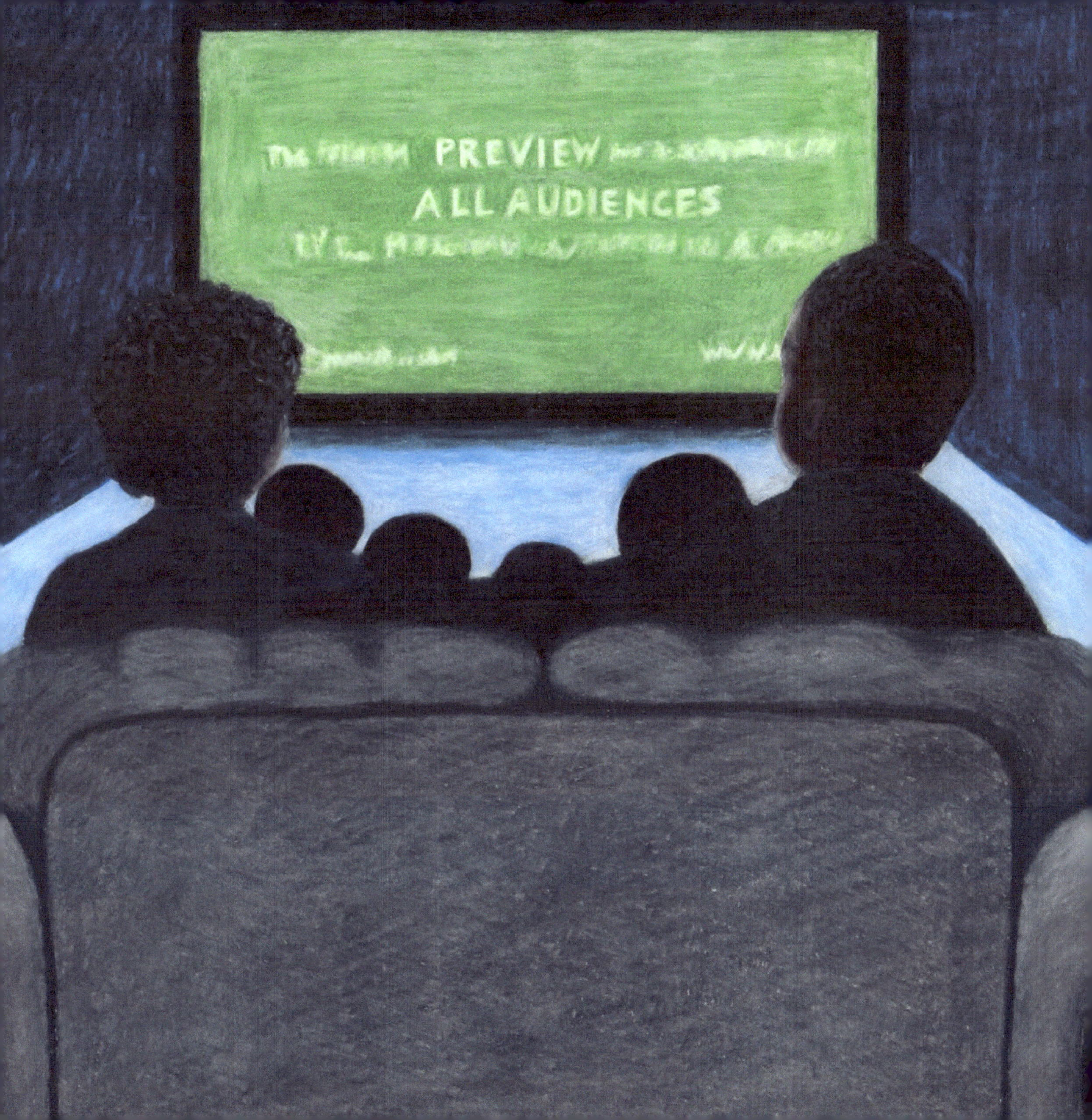
PREVIEW
ALL AUDIENCES

We play with action figures and make the cars go vroom vroom. But when we're done, we must clean up our room.

On the outside, I'm just like any other kid. I run, kick, and jump off the couch when mommy and daddy are not around. But if I get too tired, I must sit down.

My eyes can be yellow, or jaundice and my skin can look pale. The reason is because of the quick breakdown of the sickled red blood cells.

Mommy watches me to see if I feel too tired or when there is a need for surgery. I might have to get a blood transfusion, that's when they take the blood out of me.

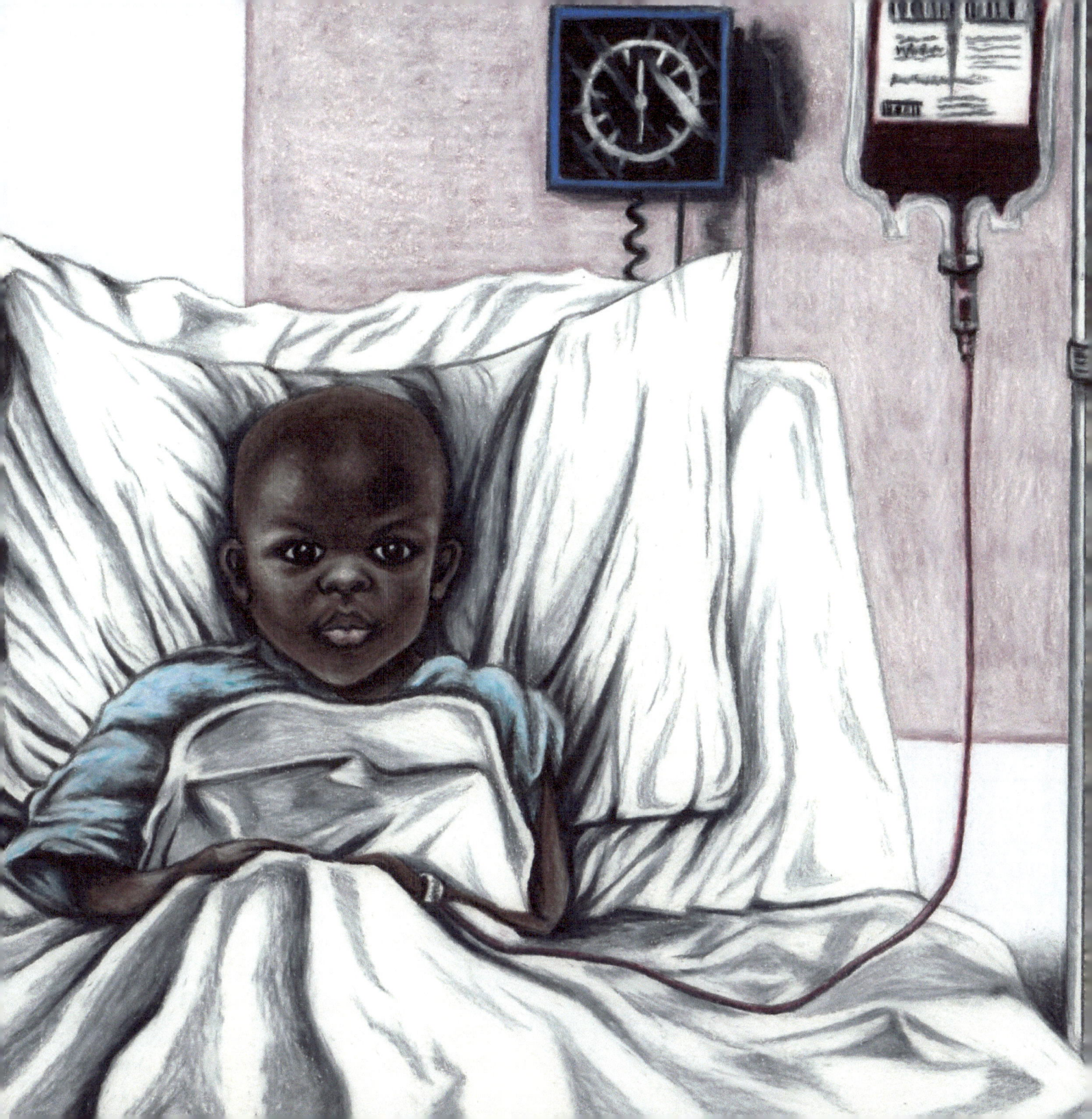

It's not so bad because normal red blood cells are the key. They put the good blood back in and I get to see Dr. Shurney.

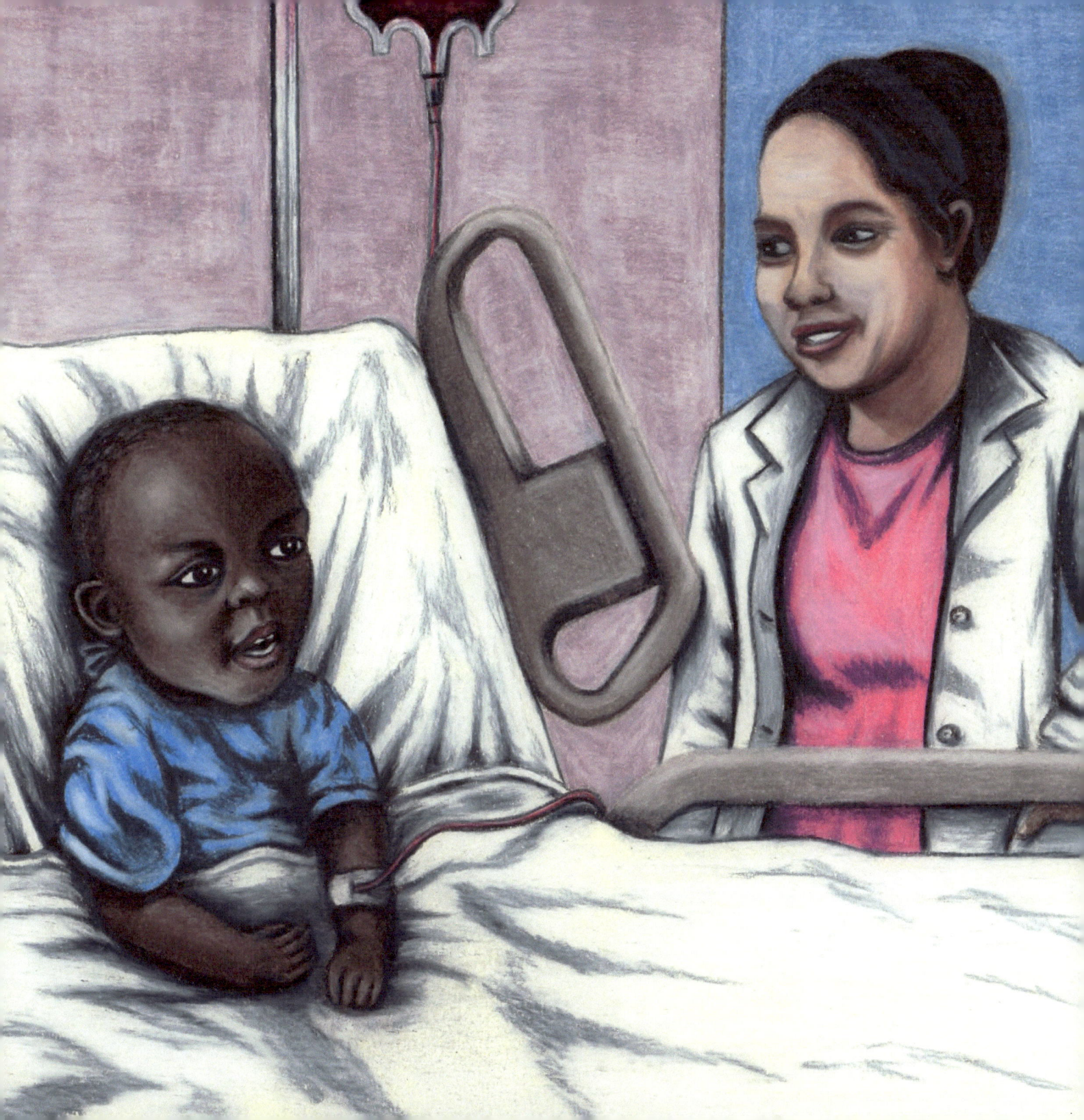

She is so nice and always makes me smile. Daddy says she is very busy and can only stay a little while.

Mommy and Daddy tell my brothers and me we can achieve anything. So, I can be whatever I want to be. Dr. Shurney told me I was a sickle cell warrior, so I won't let this disease STOP ME!

Meet the Authors

La'Shardae & Eric Scott are the parents of 2 boys who live with the lifelong illness of sickle cell disease. Their two boy's names are Emory and Evan. Emory and Evan's older brother Eric "EJ" who does not have the disease wanted to know more about his brother's illness. Because of the family's experience, La'Shardae and Eric decided to write a book to explain some of the basic information to him and others.

Meet the Illustrator

Sara Luckhardt is pursuing a Bachelor of Fine Arts degree at Eastern Michigan University. She is concentrating on watercolor, although she works in many mediums. The illustrations for this book were made with Prismacolor colored pencils. She hopes to continue illustrating books because she has a passion for reading and the narrative aspect of images.